AF504432

If Grandma Were President

Written by Pat Goldys
Illustrated by JeQuavius J. Pope

Let's vote for Grandma to be President!
She's smart,
hard working
and cares for everyone.
With these skills it's also very evident,
That she will have fun
as she gets the job done!

NDMA 2020
STRENGTH
COMPASSION 2020
CHANGE
LOVE GRANNY

Jobs will be created
to give everyone money that they need.
Schools will teach all kids
to write, problem solve and read.
Police will keep law and order
so equity will exceed.
Grandma will show
how to listen with respect
as the way to lead.

A+

Every person and animal
are created equal in every way.
Just like people
who have homes to live in each day,
All cats and dogs need a place to stay.
All will be rescued and adopted,
not even one left stray!

Free speech is important
each and everyday.
Nice words only are what we all
will hear and learn to say.
Give lots of compliments
at work and at play.
Walk the talk in the very kind
and thoughtful Grandma way!

At the WHITE HOUSE,
will be lots of exercise.
All healthy and happy is the great hope.
A treadmill and elliptical
are placed in every room.
Can't leave the tour
without a jump rope!

Grandma
will teach lessons she believes,
Will help all citizens to achieve,
A life of hope,
love and happiness,
Mixed with fun to be a real success!!

!
A
2020

There will be meetings
in the Oval Office during afternoon tea.
Just for girls aspiring to be president,
one of many we will see!
The time has come for change
in what is being done.
Grandma will cross off
the list of problems one by one.

The biggest cookoff
in food trucks all famous chefs will ride,
With all the grannies who like to cook
their secret recipes with pride,
Making delicious meals on wheels
for the homeless, elderly, and poor.
So that the days of poverty and hunger
do not exist anymore!

Freedom of dress
at meetings with the press.
No fancy suit,
high heel shoes or frilly dress.
Just comfy, cozy play clothes,
like you wear at recess!
No more worries
when we make a great big mess!

Grandma's
photo ops with families will be,
A way to promote bonding absolutely!
Families eat dinner
with Grandma President.
And take leftovers and dessert
back to their residence!

Grandma will check her budget daily,
To make sure there is enough money,
For kids' summer camps
of creative skills to study,
Like storywriting,
singing or playing the ukelele.

A B C D E F G H I J K
GO
NANA
$ $ $ $

The pursuit of happiness will be
the mission Grandma will proclaim.
Make a quilt of good laws
and rules that she will explain.
Babysit the country
so no harm will come.
That's how a Grandma's never ending love
will make the nation number 1!

Do the right thing;
learn the right stuff!
Vote! Vote! Vote!
When you are old enough!

A President is a leader
that is thoughtful and fair,
A protector of all people
defending with love and care.
A teacher of freedom,
showing what is right.
A caretaker
keeping a healthy lifestyle in sight.
A thinker working on problems to solve.
A creator whose vision and mission involves,
Building a country that happily evolves!

Grandma learned a lot from the past!
Grandma knows what the people need!
Grandma will lead us to a better future!
The grandchildren all agreed!

Dedication

To my mom and dad, Theresa and Raymond Helinski, who raised me to be a caring leader!

Pat Goldys

Pat Goldys was an educator for 39 years.
She was a teacher, assistant principal, and principal.
She is a mother of 3 grown sons and 2 daughters in law.
She has one granddaughter, Mila,
who inspires the many stories for the books!
Pat started her writing career at 64 years old and has many ideas
for future children's books.

@AuthorPatGoldys

AuthorPatGoldys@gmail.com